Dead Man's Gold

and other westerns

by
Sy Levine
and
Ray Harris

Watermill Press

Printed in the United States of America

Illustrations by Jim Odbert

ISBN 0-89375-772-1

Contents

Sharp Shot

I'm glad I left that last piece of pie on the plate, Sam Yee said to himself. *The way this stagecoach bounces, it just might make me sick.* The stage had left California two days ago, and was now in Texas.

Sam leaned his head out the window and gulped in air. Dry, Texas air — it sure felt good. It was clean air, but it was nothing at all like back home. Sam looked around. This range wasn't anything like the land back home either.

Sam thought about growing up on his father's fruit farm. It was a lush, rambling farm with trees, hills, and lots of pasture. There was even a small pond where Sam used to go fishing.

Sam had to laugh when he looked out the window again. It didn't look as if he'd be doing much fishing around here. "I must be homesick already," he muttered. "I know I'm going to miss all of those plums and pears from back home."

Then Sam thought of his family. They had put him on the coach, fussed over him, and cried a little. Sam would be gone for two years at law school in New Orleans. But he still wasn't sure he wanted to go there. He was young, maybe too young for law school.

If only I could take a year off, Sam thought. *I could work at some job, and then go to law school next year. But how can I do it?* Suddenly, the stagecoach lurched to a stop.

"Big Creek, folks," the coachman announced. "That's as far as we go today. Rest yourselves, because we start out at sunup tomorrow. All out, all out!"

Sam let out a sigh of relief. He was happy the ride was over for today. He felt stiff everywhere, and not the least bit hungry.

Sam looked out the window to see what kind of town he'd be staying in tonight. Big Creek seemed like a nice place, though it wasn't big at all. He saw a few stores, a jailhouse, and a bank.

"Big Creek, folks," the coachman announced.

Sam grabbed his cloth suitcase and headed for the hotel. He couldn't miss it. It was the only one in town. A crowd of ten or twelve had gathered in front of it. They were reading a sign posted on the wall.

SHOOT YOUR WAY INTO THE SHERIFF'S CHAIR!

BIG TARGET SHOOT
June 10th

*Get Facts at
Hotel Desk*

Sam went to the desk to get a room for the night. He asked the clerk what the sign was about.

"Brad Hearn has been the sheriff here

A crowd had gathered in front of the hotel.

since I was a boy," the desk clerk explained. "But he's getting on in years, and it's time someone took his place. That's why we're having a target shoot. Whoever gets the best score will be the new sheriff of Big Creek."

The next morning, the stagecoach for New Orleans left at dawn. But Sam Yee wasn't on it. He was oiling up his Colt single-action gun. Then he had breakfast and coffee. After he finished, he made his way over to the field where the target shoot was being held. Half the town was heading that way, too.

When Sam signed up, there were twenty men ahead of him. He watched them all shoot. Some didn't even hit the target, but others were quite good. They took aim slowly, held their hands steady as a rock, and squeezed off the shots smoothly.

One man, in a white Stetson hat, had sunk eight shots in the bull's-eye—two more than anyone else. He was the one to beat.

Now Sam was called up. It was his turn to shoot. He knelt down, drew a bead, and let go the first shot. It was close, but no bull's-eye. Sam shifted his grip a little—just a hair.

Figuring it was now or never, he fired all five shots remaining in the Colt. And they all hit the bull's-eye. The crowd held its breath.

Sam loaded four more bullets into the Colt. That made ten. And when the smoke cleared, the crowd couldn't believe it. All four shots were in the small red circle—nine out of ten! The job was Sam's.

Sam let go the first shot.

"Where did you learn to shoot like that?" the mayor of Big Creek asked him.

"Back home in Fresno, my dad has a fruit farm. He let my cousin and me put old, rotten plums and pears on the fence. We'd shoot at them. I got pretty good. But you ought to see my cousin. She's twice as good."

Everyone laughed and congratulated Sam. They wanted to say they shook the hand of the first Chinese-American sheriff in Texas.

Mule Team

Muley Scroggs and Echo Bates were looking down from the top of Goat Hill. "It's loose gravel all the way," Muley said, "slick as river ice."

"Yep. Just like river ice," Echo replied.

Muley, deep in thought, spit into the brush. Echo spit, too. They weren't saying they were scared to go down that hill. They were just a bit nervous, that was all.

Muley and Echo ran an express business. Usually, they hauled freight for the miners in the Sierras. But now, they were hauling ties for the railroad. The Central Pacific Railroad was building its line east from California. By next year, 1868, it would meet the Union Pacific, which was building west from Nebraska. When they joined the rails, the track would run all the way from the Atlantic to the Pacific. It would be a great day for America.

But before rails could be laid, wooden ties had to be put down. Muley and Echo were hauling these ties to the railroad builders. The builders would set the ties in place and wait for the rails.

The big loads went to Muley and

Echo. Muley was famous up and down the West Coast as the best muleskinner in California. Echo was famous for his great strength. Muley was small and wiry. Echo was a huge man with great, bulging muscles.

"It's a little dangerous," Muley told Echo. "But the money is good. We get $100 a load. And there's a bonus if we beat the schedule."

"Yep," Echo said. "The money is good."

Now, they were sitting on top of Goat Hill with five tons of railroad ties in a big wagon. A team of twenty mules stretched out in front of them. Muley and Echo wondered if they would get down to the railroad camp in one piece.

"Must be just about a mile down to camp," Muley guessed.

"Yep. Just about a mile," Echo agreed.

*Muley and Echo wondered if they would get
down to the railroad camp in one piece.*

"And if the brakes don't hold us on the downhill, those mules sure won't." Muley spit again and hit a twisted pine.

"No, sir, the mules sure won't," Echo agreed again. And he spit, too.

"Well, let's get it over with," Muley said at last. "I'll hang on to the brake on my side. You work the chain brake for the wheels on your side, Echo."

"Right," Echo said. "I'll work the chain brake."

Muley cracked his whip. "Gee-up, you lazy critters," he yelled to his team. The mules plunged ahead and to the right. "Now, *haw!*" he cried, and he snapped the whip again. The mules plunged to the left and the wagon began to roll.

At first, it rolled slowly. Then it went over the rim of the hill and tilted downward. Both men pulled on the brake

19

levers. The wheels locked and held. The wagon slid in the loose gravel at about the same speed that the mules traveled. Things were going smoothly.

And that's the way it was supposed to stay till they got down to the camp. Unfortunately, that's not what happened.

First, a horsefly landed on Echo's nose. Echo didn't dare let go of the brake. He wiggled his nose, but the fly stayed on. It seemed to enjoy the scenery. Echo stuck out his bottom lip and blew. The fly just cooled itself in the breeze. Echo tried sneezing, but that got the fly mad. It bit Echo so hard, it drew blood. Then Echo howled so loud, the mules were frightened and started running. At the same time, Echo let go of the brake to swat the fly.

Because the hill was so steep, the

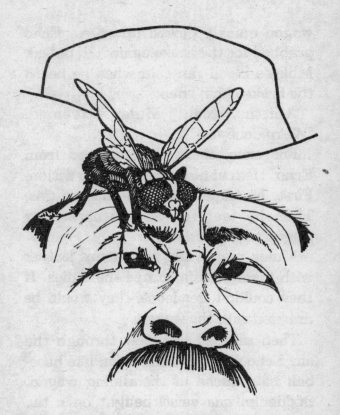

A horsefly landed on Echo's nose.

wagon quickly picked up speed. Echo grabbed for the brake again and pulled. Muley's blood ran cold when he heard the brake chain snap.

"Oh, my gosh!" Muley screamed. "We're done for!"

For once, there was no echo from Echo. He had already gone into action. First, he leaped onto the load of ties. Then he teetered as the careening wagon turned sideways.

Muley, meanwhile, was cutting leather with his big knife to free the mules. If they couldn't get loose, they would be dragged with the wagon.

Then railroad ties flew through the air. Echo was throwing them like baseball bats ahead of the sliding wagon. Suddenly, one wheel caught on a tie. Then another caught. A mound of loose gravel grew ahead of the ties and wagon. And still, the wagon slid.

Echo kept throwing ties. Soon the ties piled up, and the gravel piled up, and the mules piled up. Finally, the wagon began to slow. It slowed, but it didn't stop.

In the railroad camp, the first thing the workers saw was a cloud of dust. Then someone shouted, "Avalanche! Run for your lives!" But there was no time to run as the avalanche of gravel, mules, and ties came sliding into camp. It crashed into the cook shack and ground to a halt.

One by one, the mules shook themselves loose. Within minutes, twenty mules were running in twenty different directions. The camp foreman ran to see what had caused the commotion. When he saw the mess, his face turned red with rage. "Who is responsible for this?" he demanded.

Echo was too busy looking for Muley to answer. "Muley!" he called. "Muley! Where are you?"

There was a faint sound from under a heap of ties and gravel. Echo dove into the pile. Ties flew and gravel flew until Muley's slim shape appeared in the rubble.

"It's about time you got this mess off of me," Muley said. "Now, who is the boss around here?" he asked, looking around.

The camp foreman stepped forward. At the moment, he was swearing he would have someone's hide for this.

Muley found his hat and dusted himself off with it. "That will be $100, cash," he said, "for one load of railroad ties

*Ties flew and gravel flew until Muley's slim
shape appeared in the rubble.*

delivered on site." He took a bill from his boot and handed it to the foreman.

"Cash," Echo repeated for his partner. And he held out his big hand to receive the money. "Plus a $20 bonus. We were ahead of schedule."

Buffalo Sal

You can see the sign for fifteen miles in any direction:

EAT AT BUFFALO SAL'S

The Burger Queen

Sal's is clear out in the middle of nowhere, it seems. That's why you can see

Sal's is clear out in the middle of nowhere.

her sign from so far away. It's halfway between Carvel and Spring Lake on the old road to Tucson. No one travels that way anymore since they built the interstate. But Sal stays on and manages to make a living.

The local folks still come in for pie and coffee. And if they feel reckless, they buy a hamburger. The sheriff always stops by on his rounds. And sometimes, a stray trucker will come down from the interstate looking for a bargain meal.

Sal makes good pie and coffee. But if the truth were known, her hamburgers are awful. That's how she got her nickname, "Buffalo" Sal.

It was right after Sheriff Bean got his new teeth. Some of the boys were sitting around chewing on Sal's hamburgers when the sheriff came in. Let me tell you, Sal's hamburgers take a lot of chewing. They're tough as old saddle leather and dry as sawdust. But nobody would ever say anything. They didn't want to hurt Sal's feelings.

So the sheriff came in and smiled. He wanted everybody to admire his new teeth. And just to show off, he ordered a hamburger.

Maybe it was the hamburger. Or maybe the dentist didn't fit the teeth very well. But when the sheriff took his first bite and took the burger out of his mouth, the teeth came with it. There they were, still biting the hamburger.

Early Jones, a sheepherder, choked on the peach pie he was swallowing at the time. And Abel Murphy laughed so hard, he fell off his stool. You can bet the sheriff was mad.

"Blast it, Sal," the sheriff spluttered. "It's time someone told you. You make the worst hamburgers in Arizona—maybe in the whole United States. If I didn't know better, I'd think you made them from old buffalo hide."

Ever since then, she was known as Buffalo Sal. And her friends chipped in to make the sign I told you about.

But I'm getting away from my story. That was the day two strangers stopped by Sal's.

Sal was alone at the time. None of the regulars was around. And these two men drove up in an old Chevy van. Sal didn't like their looks, but she never turned away customers.

The regulars always sat at the counter. But these two sat at the one table Sal had by the window. They kept looking

*The sheriff wanted everybody to admire his
new teeth.*

down the road. It was as if they expected someone. Or maybe they were on the run, Sal thought. So she made sure her old .44 was in its place under the counter.

One of the strangers, a big blubbery fellow, smiled at Sal. "What have you got today, Grandma?" he asked.

Sal pointed to the blackboard on the wall. She ignored the man's nasty tone.

There wasn't much and the men read quickly—two kinds of homemade soup, Sal's special hamburgers, hash made from yesterday's hamburgers, apple pie, and coffee.

The other fellow, a tall and lanky guy, grunted. "Is that all you have?"

Sal nodded. She hoped they would leave, but they didn't.

"OK," the lanky one said. "Give us two

hamburgers, apple pie, and coffee. And we're in a hurry. So move it!"

"Yes, sir," Sal said. But for spite, she didn't move very fast at all. She shuffled over to the freezer and got out her roll of hamburger. I say it was a roll because that's the way she kept it. It was about two feet long and four inches across, like a big salami. She kept it frozen solid. Then she would cut off slices for hamburger patties as she needed them. Now she cut off two and threw them on the grill. She left the rest of the roll on her sandwich board. She'd put it away when she was through serving.

She cooked the hamburgers, cut the pie, and poured the coffee. Sal made coffee range style, the way they used to on cattle drives. She put the grounds in a huge coffeepot and boiled them. Then she threw in eggshells to settle the grounds. Add a pinch of salt, and it was done. It was very hot and very strong.

The fat man choked on Sal's coffee. "Are you trying to poison us, Grandma?" he growled. Sal said nothing.

"Just eat and let's get out of here, Frank," the tall one said. Sal watched him watch the road.

They finished quickly and walked to the counter. "That'll be two and a half dollars," Sal said.

The fat man reached into his jeans and came up with a nickel-plated revolver. "It's on the house, Grandma," he said. "And for trying to poison us, we'll just take what you've got in the cash register."

No one is sure what happened next. Sal would never tell that part. But when Sheriff Bean got there, the two men

*"We'll just take what you've got
in the cash register."*

were on the floor, out cold. Sal was standing over them with her .44.

It turned out that they had just robbed a bank in Silver City. The loot was still in the van. So Sal got her picture in the paper and everything. Of course, the reporters wanted to know how she did it.

"I got the drop on them," was all she would say. "Never mind how."

Sheriff Bean was no Sherlock Holmes. But he was a good policeman, and he noticed things. For example, the fat man had a burned hand. There was coffee spilled on the floor. Both men had egg-sized lumps on their heads. And Sal's roll of hamburger was thawing on the counter.

"I calculate," he said to me later, then he had to stop to laugh. "I calculate that when the fat guy pulled his gun, Sal poured coffee on his hand. She keeps that big pot of hers next to the cash register. Then she must have hit them both with her roll of frozen hamburger."

"You're kidding," I said.

"No, I'm not," the sheriff laughed. "And if I were you, next time you're in Sal's, order the hash. It's a day old, but at least it isn't a dangerous weapon."

Jake Dean's Dream

Jake Dean says he knew it was there all along. But to tell you the truth, he was just plain lucky.

He came to Texas many years ago. And when he got to Austin, he told the whole town why he'd come.

"Friends and neighbors," Jake said in his booming voice, "I'm a farmer. I've come to the West to do what I do best. Yes, sir, I had the biggest and proudest apple farm in the state of New York. And I've come to grow apples in Texas."

Well, we just laughed. And when Jake Dean bought the old Simmons place, we laughed even harder.

You've got to understand something about the old Simmons place. It was the driest, most sun-baked piece of earth this side of Death Valley.

Old Man Simmons had tried to run a ranch on that land, but he couldn't keep his stock watered. There just wasn't enough water to be found. So, Old Man Simmons moved on. He told Curly Bates down at the bank to sell the place to any fool that would buy it.

Well, Jake heard about the Simmons

*"I had the biggest apple farm in the
state of New York."*

41

place and wanted to see it. Curly took Jake out for a look, figuring Jake would do what all the others had done—take one look at that piece of scorched toast and say no.

But Jake didn't say no. He walked around the land, looked at the sky, and checked the wind's direction. Then he smiled at Curly Bates.

"Yes, sir, I'll buy this piece of land. It smells like success. And that's a mighty good smell to my way of thinking."

Curly shook his head a few times. He'd seen and heard a lot of fools in his time, but Jake Dean was definitely the biggest of them all. "You're sure?" he asked Jake.

"Sure, I'm sure," Jake boomed. "Now, let's get back to town so I can sign the deed."

Curly took Jake back to the bank and drew up the deed. Jake paid in cash and signed the paper with a happy smile.

"Welcome to Austin," Curly said. "It's a pleasure to do business with you, Mr. Dean."

"Call me Jake," the farmer said. "You think I'm out of my mind, don't you?"

"Uh, not exactly," Curly lied.

"You've got to trust your instincts. That's what my old Daddy used to say — trust your instincts. Now, I've got to get moving. I've got a well to dig."

Jake dug his first well that very week. We got used to seeing him come to town for supplies, baked from the sun and covered with the worthless dirt he'd bought.

Jake would storm into the general store and pound his fists on the counter.

Jake paid in cash with a happy smile.

"More pipe! Come on, time's a-wasting. I'm getting close to the water, friends and neighbors. I can feel it."

Then he'd load the pipe onto his old truck. You always knew it was Jake Dean's truck. It didn't have a muffler. And it sure did make a lot of noise. Even from far away, you could hear it go, "chug-bang-cough-BOOM!"

After a while, folks in Austin stopped laughing at Jake Dean. As it turned out, he was a mighty nice fellow, and folks began to feel more than a little sorry about Jake and his apple farm.

"Poor Jake Dean," they said. "Why, he's as blind as a man can be. There isn't any water on that land. What little there was, Old Man Simmons used up. Jake would be better off trying to mix concrete with all that sand he has."

Jake dug three wells that first spring. Of course, they were dry. But dry wells didn't seem to bother Jake. He would just order more pipe.

It was right after well Number Seven proved dry that folks saw a change in Jake. When Jake came to town, he looked exhausted. He didn't yell quite so loud anymore, and even his truck didn't make as much noise.

One day, Jake sat in front of the store with a bunch of his friends and took a rest from his digging. "I've got the most stubborn piece of land in Texas," he said. "I know there's water down there. My land knows I know, too."

Jake had a strange way of talking about his land as if it were a person. He'd call his land names, and then he would apologize.

"Are you about ready to give up, Jake?" one of the boys asked.

"I'm just about ready," Jake said. "I'm going to try one more time. To tell you the truth, friends, I could use a favor."

Jake asked them to come out to his place, just for luck. So, a bunch of them followed Jake to the last well site.

Jake owned a big piece of land. And, except for a small patch near the house, it was covered with well sites. The place looked kind of funny with all of those holes. But nobody laughed now.

"This well has got to go deeper than the rest," Jake said. "I think that's been the problem."

But Jake couldn't have picked a worse site for the well. The ground was hard and rocky, which made the drilling go slowly.

In a few days, Jake had drilled down as deep as the rest of his wells. There still wasn't a hint of water. But that didn't surprise anybody.

Jake tried to dig deeper, but the drill hit hard rock. It stopped moving and made a whirring sound. It sure looked as though it were the end of Jake Dean's dream.

Well, Jake got riled up at that point. He stomped around the well, then he climbed on the rigging and yelled at his land.

"Listen to me, you sorry piece of dirt! I'm going to grow apples here, and you're going to help. Do you hear?"

Jake went back to his drill and hit it a few times with a wrench. Then he started the drill motor again. The drill eased into the ground and stopped. But a moment later, it moved and kept going.

The ground trembled and groaned near the well. Jake didn't know what to expect next. Nobody did.

KA-BOOM!

The ground trembled some more. Then a huge, black spray shot out of the pipe.

"What the heck is that?" Jake yelled. "Swamp water, I bet. Who needs swamp water?" Jake wanted water so badly, he wasn't thinking straight.

"It's oil, you fool!" the boys shouted. "You've struck oil, Jake!"

The boys tapped the pipe to stop the flow of the oil, and watched Jake wander around the site. They could see he was thinking hard.

"Oil?" he said. "You know, boys, this just might be a good thing."

Now the boys had to laugh. It looked

A huge black spray shot out of the pipe.

as if Jake Dean wasn't as crazy as everyone had thought.

A few days later, an oil company came from Dallas and told Jake they'd like to try a few more wells. With their special equipment, it seemed like a good idea.

Jake told them to go ahead and try. But he also told them not to dig near his patch of land by the house. "I've got plans for that," he said.

The Dallas folks found oil in two more of Jake's wells. And that made him a rich man.

We expected to see Jake riding around in a fancy new car, but no one saw him at all for two weeks. As it turned out, Jake had one more surprise for Austin.

Jake took his oil money back up to New York, where he bought a neighbor's apple farm. He hired two huge trucks and filled them with the topsoil from the farm. In one of the trucks, he put five tiny apple trees. Then he brought the trees and dirt back to Austin.

Jake cleared his old house off his land and planted the topsoil. He placed the apple trees in the center of the new land. But he wasn't through yet.

He had his oil crew lay a pipe all the way to Lake Travis. Now he had water and good soil for his apples.

It took a couple of years, but Jake did make apples grow in Texas.

"Friends and neighbors," he liked to say, "I was lucky. There's no doubt about that. But you've got to remember one thing. Where there's a well, there's a way."

Eight Dry Bones

"Pass the corn, May Rose. And don't sit there dreaming," her father said. "What are you thinking about, anyway?"

"Nothing, Pa," May Rose replied. "But I'm worried about what you and Ma were just saying. If it doesn't rain soon, the whole herd might die. Pa, that would be an awful thing to happen to

"If it doesn't rain soon, the whole herd might die."

those poor cows — and to the calves."

"It'd be awful for us, too, child," her mother said solemnly.

"That's why I want to bring Dark Elk home. He told me about rainmaking while we were waiting for class to start. He says his grandfather is a famous chief. And his grandfather taught Dark Elk how to make rain. He says when a Hopi..."

"May Rose, I don't want to hear another word of that nonsense. I don't care what a Hopi chief says. When it's time to have rain, we'll have it. And when it isn't, we've just got to sit here and wait until it is."

After supper was finished and she did her chores on their small ranch, May Rose heard her parents talking. Her mother was taking May Rose's side!

"It's doesn't matter if that Hopi boy can make it rain, or if he can't," her mother was saying. "I don't say he can. In fact, Joe, I know he can't. But he's *her* friend. And she wants to help us."

The next morning, before school, May Rose's father was in the barn. Her mother said to May Rose, "Oh, child, if you feel like asking your friend to come by, go ahead. I'd be glad to see him."

That afternoon, May Rose watched Dark Elk as he got his rainmaking things ready. He stood under a pine tree in front of the cabin.

Dark Elk cleared away a circle in the pine needles on the ground and brought over a big, flat stone. Then he opened a deerskin bag and took out eight small, dry bones. He arranged the bones in a ring on the stone.

*Dark Elk arranged the bones in a ring
on the stone.*

While May Rose watched, Dark Elk stood up and raised his arms. He sang a long, tuneless song to the Great Spirit. Then he picked up the bones and arranged them in a square shape.

At last, Dark Elk danced around the stone eight times. He was so quiet, May Rose couldn't hear him. Then he passed his hands over the bones, picked them up and put them back in the bag.

Dark Elk said good-bye to May Rose and her mother, and walked home.

At supper that night, no one said a word about the Hopi boy's visit. They talked about May Rose's cousin, and some news from town. But they said nothing about the rain.

When May Rose was in bed, she heard her father ask if Dark Elk had come. Her mother said yes. Then her father

That's thunder, *May Rose thought.*
Sure enough, thunder!

replied, "That's a foolish thing to do. I don't see the use of teaching that girl such nonsense. But it's done now, so we'd best forget it."

May Rose thought her father wasn't fair to Dark Elk. *He doesn't even know the Hopis, so how could he know if. . .* Just then, she heard a loud, booming noise. It sounded like a gun. Then she heard it again, nearer.

That's no gun, May Rose thought. *That's* thunder. *Sure enough, thunder! And what's that other sound? That's . . .* rain! *On the roof of our cabin—rain! Let's see what Pa says in the morning,* she thought as she fell asleep.

The _New_ Old Days

"What took you so long to get the mail?" Joe's father asked. "Did you have a shoot-out with some rustlers by the mailbox?"

"Ha, ha, very funny," Joe Bayles said. "But I could have been back a lot sooner if I had a horse."

"I could have been back a lot sooner if I had a horse," Joe said.

"Now, Joe, don't start that. There's no use pestering me about that again. I told you before, you're living in modern times — not back in the old days."

"But, Dad, we need a horse for a lot of things. Now that we live on a ranch . . ."

His father finished repairing the hinge on the barn door. "This is a farm, Joe, not a ranch. I've told you that a dozen times. Besides, we have enough to do without taking care of a horse. The jeep and tractor are all we need."

Joe knew he'd gone as far as he could, so he dropped the subject. There was no use bugging his Dad. When Mr. Bayles said no, he meant it.

All that summer, the TV news ran stories about big problems in far-off Middle Eastern countries. The announcers explained that most of our oil comes from the Middle East. They showed pictures of gas stations, in all parts of America, with long lines of cars waiting their turn to fill up.

Mr. Bayles waited, too. He would drive the jeep into town, then wait an hour to fill it up. That was an hour he wasn't working—an hour wasted. He had to go back out in the fields after supper to get things done.

Still, Joe said nothing.

On his way back from one of those long waits in town, Joe's father met an old friend, Doc Kraus. He passed him on the road and pulled over to wait for Doc to catch up. Doc was on horseback.

"Oh, it's you, Doc," Mr. Bayles laughed. "I thought it was one of those movie cowboys."

"I hear jokes like that a lot," Doc

Joe's father pulled over to wait for Doc.

smiled, "but I never pay much attention. The ones who tease me are paying *six times* what they used to pay for gas. And they're lucky if they can even get it, at any price. This horse doesn't drink much gas at all, Bayles."

"Where did you buy him?" Joe's father asked.

"Right in town," said Doc.

The two men talked for a while longer, and then each went his own way. When Mr. Bayles got home, he called Joe into the kitchen. They sat at the table.

"Joe, when you get to be my age, you'll have your own kids. And you'll learn there's one thing that's a lot better than being right."

"What's that, Dad?" Joe asked.

"It's when your kid is right. And that's how I feel now. You were right all along about our needing a horse. There's only one thing you were wrong about—we need *two* horses.

"So you sit right there," his father said. "I want you to hear me ordering *our* horses. Is that what you had in mind?"

Joe didn't have to answer. His grin spoke louder than words.

Dead Man's Gold

Nights were scary for Nan Holt. Since her mother and father were killed last year in a wagon crash, Nan and her two brothers lived alone on the ranch, twelve miles from any town.

In the daytime, they worked the ranch. Two cowhands rode in from New Rome to help them. But when the hands left at sundown, Nan and her brothers were alone again.

The howl of a wolf or the low moaning of the wind didn't spook Nan. She grew up on the range and was used to these sounds. They were natural. When it stormed, and thunder shook the house, she wasn't frightened. "Let it boom all it wants to," she'd say. "We need the rain."

But something else made Nan Holt shiver, turning her hands and toes as cold as ice. Sounds that she didn't know could frighten her—like the sound out there right now. It wasn't a horse or the wind. It was a person. Some stranger was there in the yard, creeping in the shadows. To do what? *Why is he there?* she wondered.

Nan never liked to let her brothers, Tom and Todd, know when she was

Some stranger was there in the yard.

frightened. She was the one in charge. She ought to be able to handle any problem. But this was different. The situation was too much for her. If there really was someone lurking out there, it would take all three of them to fight.

"Wake up, men," she called into their room. "Put your boots and clothes on, but don't light any candles. We've got ourselves a problem."

In a minute, they were dressed and sitting next to their sister. She made them listen quietly, and then they heard it, too. Someone was out there, all right. They heard a clunk and a clank, as if someone were digging.

Todd made a quick plan. The three of them would sneak outside slowly, on tiptoes. Without a sound, Todd would go all the way around the house, to the right. Tom would go round the other way, to the left. Nan would wait a moment and then come running straight at the stranger. Whoever it was would think he was surrounded.

Tom and Nan would carry the two rifles. Todd would use their father's old army sword. And they'd yell and scare the daylights out of the stranger.

That's just what they did. War whoops and screams woke the livestock and the dogs. The animals helped make even more of a racket. It was the loudest noise ever heard on the prairie.

The stranger dropped his shovel, then dropped down on the ground beside it. He was surprised and shaking. Nan and the boys rushed in and grabbed him.

"Wait, you two," Tom yelled. "I know this guy. It's Old Red. He hangs around the stables in town, always telling stories about his days as a gold miner."

By this time, the red-bearded old man was back on his feet. "Lay off, you kids," he yelled, "I haven't harmed you. I'd never hurt the sprouts of old Dan Holt."

When they heard Old Red mention their father's name, the Holt kids were quiet. Then Nan said, "If you knew our Pa, Mister Red, why are you here, in the middle of the night, digging up our land?"

"Shoot, Miss Nan, haven't you heard? Your Pa and I were partners, back in the old times. We were gold miners—and good ones, at that. Those other fools, they dug themselves sick, and never found one ounce of the stuff. But your Pa and I spent five hard months in the hills. At the end of that time, we hit it big." Old Red held out a sack. "We filled this bag with yellow dust. We were rich men."

The old man sat down on the ground in the moonlight and started to laugh. It made him feel happy thinking about all that gold. A few minutes later, he continued his story.

"But then the price of gold dropped way down. It was down so low, your Pa and I had to do something. So we made a plan. We hid the sack of gold in a hole under this tree."

The old man went on. "We were going to leave it here for a year, or maybe five years, till the price of gold came back up. Then your poor Pa and Ma got themselves killed."

Tom interrupted, "So you reckoned you'd come back here, dig it up, and

"We filled this bag with yellow dust,"
Old Red said.

disappear with it. We're sure lucky we caught you. You're a fine partner, you are, stealing from a dead man—and his kids!"

The old man was shocked. "You think I'd do that, Tommy? Then you don't know Old Red, you don't. Why, I came here to dig up this gold, that's true. But I was going to give you kids half. That's what belongs to you rightfully. I wouldn't have it any other way."

After a short spell, Nan said, "I believe you, Mister Red. Come on in the house, out of the cold, and don't forget to bring that sack with you. Now that we're all rich, I'm going to make us a cake, a nice six-egg cake—right now, in the middle of the night."

Tom and Todd were more than glad to help Old Red with the heavy bag of gold dust. He laughed to himself as he wiped his hands on his filthy shirt. It wasn't often he was invited into a clean home like the Holt cabin. And never, in all his long years, had a girl baked a cake for him in the middle of the night. Old Red would have plenty to tell his friends when he got back to town.

Ride Quick—
I'm Dying!

No cowhand ever worked on the range with his shirt off. The sun could be scorching, but the shirt stayed on. If you looked at a cowpuncher's back and chest, even after he had spent a year in the blazing sun, you'd never see a tan.

Today was a real scorcher. Brad

punched cows on Judge Brown's ranch. It was a huge spread. Brad had started out in the cool dawn, about six hours ago. He rode his bay, Squaw, straight out to Los Pardos, the hilly range where the grass was thick and high. That's where the cows and calves liked to feed in this heat.

Brad was branding calves with his work partner, Jeff. It was tough, back-breaking work, and with the heat from the fire for the branding iron, Brad was doubly hot. But still, his shirt stayed on. So did his hat.

"Someone's in a big rush to get here," Jeff drawled, poking his thumb toward a rider's cloud of dust in the distance.

Mary, the judge's head cook, was under the cloud. She pulled up her horse, fanned herself with her hat, and yelled,

"Brad, Miss Beth needs you. She says to tell you to ride quick—she's dying. She says..."

But Brad didn't stay around to hear. He leaped up, put his toe in Squaw's stirrup, and swung into the saddle. A flick of his hat on Squaw's rump, and they were streaking toward the ranch house.

Brad got there quickly. Beth must have seen him tearing up to the back porch, for she shouted, "In here, Brad! Quick, in the kitchen!"

Brad charged up the steps and through the door—and then he stopped. There was Beth, up on a chair, pointing down at the kitchen floor.

"Watch out, don't let him get you, Brad. But please...do something before he jumps up here. He'll kill me!"

Brad took one look and started to

*Brad leaped up, put his foot in Squaw's
stirrup, and swung into the saddle.*

cough loudly. When he tried to stop the whoops of laughter rising in his throat, he coughed instead. And he didn't want to be rude to Miss Beth, who was Judge Brown's niece.

"The only way he'll kill you is if you stay up there on that chair for a week, Miss Beth. You'll starve yourself to death by that time. And that will make me one sad cowhand, should it happen," Brad told her.

"Please get that monster out of here," she begged him. She pointed to the ugliest, fiercest animal she'd ever seen.

"I guess they don't have horned toads back in New York, where you come from. They sure are wild-looking devils," Brad said.

While he was talking, he took off his hat. He bent over and picked up the

"Horned toads sure are wild-looking devils,"
Brad said.

83

horned toad in one hand. Then he flipped the "monster" into his hat.

"You see, that's how he protects himself, Miss Beth," he told her. "This creature is so mean-looking, folks won't mess with him. They think he'll kill them."

Brad helped Miss Beth step down. He kind of liked the softness of her arm and the way her hair smelled.

"I'm sorry I made such a fool of myself," she said, smiling. "Can I give you some lemonade to cool you off?"

"That would be nice of you, ma'am," Brad said. "But first, I'll just step outside and send this toad on his way."

Brad never did find out if Miss Beth was really scared—or whether she had found a new way to get to know a handsome cowhand.

Fouled-Up Holdup

Chris Hardy and his pal, Tim, had only been on the job for three months. They started on the day the new train line made its first run, from Utah to Texas.

The banks that owned the railroad had hired the two best shots they could find to guard the train—Chris and Tim. But they were more than great gun handlers. These two young marshals were also smart. They used their brains before they reached for their guns.

The train whistle blew to begin the trip south. Chris and Tim leaped on board as the engine built up its steam.

"Did you check all of our gear?" Chris asked his friend.

"I sure did—I double-checked it," Tim said. "I always tell you, it sure pays to be careful, just as it pays to keep your eyes open."

They walked through the passenger cars. The cars were not very crowded, but the trip was just getting under way.

Chris and Tim sat together at the back of the lead car. They leaned back and watched the view through the window.

"This is one heck of a pretty ride," Chris said. "Let's hope it stays this quiet all the way to El Paso."

The train made its first stop at Bugle Gap. Since it was a small town, the marshals knew there wouldn't be many new riders. Sure enough, just one new rider came on board, a large man in a green suit. He huffed and puffed as he came into the car. Chris and Tim watched the man take his seat. In a few moments, the man was sound asleep.

Tim walked up and down the train to see if anyone had come on board that they hadn't seen. "All clear," he announced when he returned to his seat.

The train passed through a wide valley. In the distance, the marshals could see the tips of the Sierra Ancha Mountains.

At the next stop, a large family came on board. Soon, there were kids playing all over the train. Their shouts echoed through the cars. The man in the green suit woke up with a sudden jerk. He looked around, mumbled to himself, and fell back asleep.

"I knew the quiet wouldn't last long," Tim said with a grin.

"You're right about that, partner. Do you want the first watch?" Chris asked.

Since the train ran all night, the marshals took turns getting a little rest. "Nope," Tim said, "I'm going to get some shuteye. I'll be up soon."

It was morning when the train stopped for coal at the tiny town of Silver Stone. Just as it started up again, six men wearing Navajo blankets climbed up the steps. They walked through the car where Chris and Tim were sitting.

Three spread out and sat down, while the other three walked through to the

The marshals took turns getting a little rest.

next car. Chris whispered, "Keep your
eye on those three Navajos in there. But
don't let on you're doing it."

The train had bumped and rattled
four or five miles when Chris saw his
three Navajos nod their heads at each
other. Then they slipped masks on their
faces. At the same time, they stood up
and dropped their blankets. Now they
were dressed like common gunslingers.
And each had a six-shooter in his hand.

But Chris Hardy moved even more
quickly than these three bandits. In an
instant, he was standing on his seat
with a Colt in each hand. He fired a shot
at the crook down at one end of the car.
The bullet hit the bandit on the shoul-
der, and he dropped to the floor. He was
out of the game. "You other two," Chris
yelled. "Drop your guns, or you won't be

as lucky as your friend. Do it, or you'll be two sad snakes, I promise you."

They saw that Chris meant business, so they dropped their guns. Chris marched them into the baggage car. He was joined by Tim and the other three prisoners. Chris and Tim locked the crooks in with the mail and baggage. When the train got to El Paso, they turned the six men over to the sheriff.

The man dressed in the green suit approached Chris. "My name is Frank Vaughan," he said. "My bank owns a piece of this railroad. I was in that car and saw the whole thing. May I ask you a question?"

"Why, sure, Mr. Vaughan. Ask away," Chris smiled.

"You guys reacted quickly when those crooks made their move. It seems as if

Chris marched them into the baggage car.

you suspected them all along."

"I didn't *suspect*, Mr. Vaughan—I knew! Those were Navajo blankets those snakes were wearing, but they weren't Navajos. These men had short hair, and I never saw a Navajo with short hair.

"But that wasn't the clincher," Chris Hardy continued. "I've got a brother who once spent a month's pay on a new pair of boots. They had this special kind of stitching on them. I never saw anything else quite like it. The only place you can get them is in this boot shop in Kansas City."

"Yes, but what does that have to do with these train robbers?" Frank Vaughan asked.

"Just this—when those fleabag crooks walked past me, I saw two of tnem had on those Kansas City boots. Now that

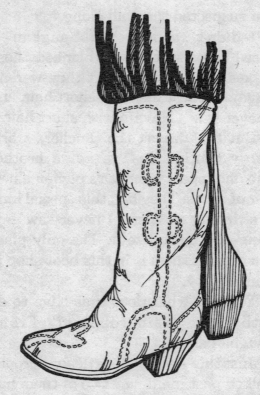

"I saw two of them had on those Kansas City boots," Chris said.

boot store is about five hundred miles from the Navajo homeland. That's a long way to travel for a pair of boots. I just *knew* we were in for trouble when I spotted those boots."